animal p

Puppy Rescue Riddle

Catherine Nichols
Illustrated by **Bryan Langdo**

Silver Dolphin

Silver Dolphin Books
An imprint of Printers Row Publishing Group
A division of Readerlink Distribution Services, LLC
9717 Pacific Heights Blvd, San Diego, CA 92121
www.silverdolphinbooks.com

Printers Row Publishing Group is a division of Readerlink Distribution Services, LLC.
Silver Dolphin Books is a registered trademark of Readerlink Distribution Services, LLC.

All notations of errors or omissions should be addressed to Silver Dolphin Books, Editorial
Department, at the above address.

All photography @ iStockphoto

ISBN: 978-1-64517-731-9
Manufactured, printed, and assembled in Shaoguan, China.
First printing, February 2021. SL/02/21
25 24 23 22 21 1 2 3 4 5

animal planet™

Puppy Rescue Riddle

PUPPY LOVE

Dogs don't speak, but they show how they feel. Some dogs love to be petted, and others like to have their ears rubbed. Your dog may want to cuddle up with you, run around and play, or just hang out.

A Change of Plans

Elliot Flynn looked out his bedroom window. It was a gray, windy Saturday. Gold leaves fell from the beech tree in front of his house and drifted across the lawn. Across the street, two girls were playing a game of catch. Elliot knew their names. Amy Chang and Kyung Lee were in his class. They both seemed nice, even if Amy always had to be right. But he only knew them enough to say hi.

They weren't his friends.

Since school had started in September, he hadn't made one friend. And now it was the end of October. What if he never had anyone to play with? Elliot wished his family had never moved to North Carolina. He had liked his old neighborhood in Virginia just fine.

He let the curtain fall back and sighed. Just then, his brother stepped into the room. Sam had his jacket on and was whistling.

"Are you going out?" Elliot asked his older brother.

"It's almost noon," Sam said. "Time to go to my job."

Sam worked part-time at Adopt-Your-BFF Dog Shelter. He was going to be a

vet when he finished school. Sam
loved all animals, but he especially
loved dogs.

"What about me?" Elliot asked.
Their parents were at a movie, and Sam
was supposed to be watching him.

Sam tossed a jacket at his brother.
"You're coming with me."

"Do I have to?" Elliot had planned
to spend the afternoon sorting his rock
collection. Yesterday he had found a
glittery rock with streaks of purple in it.

"Yes," Sam said. "You're only in
second grade. You can't stay home by
yourself."

Elliot made a face. But he put on his
jacket anyway.

• POPULAR PETS •

Some people prefer dogs to cats. Other people share their homes with fish, birds, and reptiles. Luckily, there are all kinds of pets for all kinds of people.

House cats are hunters, just like lions and tigers. The difference is that smaller cats hunt smaller animals—or catnip toys!

Big or tiny, furry or hairless, long ears or short, dogs come in all shapes and sizes. They are the number one pet in the United States.

The common goldfish, if properly cared for, can grow to be over a foot long. It can weigh as much as 4 pounds.

A guinea pig makes a good first pet because it's easy to care for. Its teeth never stop growing, so it needs hard things to chew on.

Soft and fluffy, with long, floppy ears, rabbits make great pets. You can even teach a rabbit to fetch and to use a litter box.

Turtles may be slow, but they live a long time. A box turtle can live up to forty years.

Outside, Sam and Elliot headed for a
white van. The van belonged to the shelter.

Sam used it on weekends
to pick up supplies.

As Sam unlocked the van,
a ball bounced across the street.
"Catch it!" Kyung and Amy
called out.

"Hello," Sam said, turning toward the girls.

"Hi," Kyung answered. She waved shyly to Elliot.

"Are you going to the shelter?" Amy asked. Amy loved dogs too. At school all she ever talked about was dogs, dogs, dogs.

Sam nodded. "But first I have to stop and buy puppy kibble. We just got some puppies, and they need special food."

Amy's and Kyung's eyes lit up when Sam said puppies.

"Puppies!" Amy clapped her hands. "Can we go with you to see them? Please? Pretty please?"

"We won't be any trouble," Kyung promised. "Remember when I came to the shelter to adopt Snowball?"

TAKING CARE

A doctor who treats animals is called a veterinarian, or vet for short. Some vets care for pets, such as dogs, cats, and rabbits. Other vets look after farm animals, such as sheep, goats, and horses. And vets who work in zoos keep elephants, tigers, and all the other animals healthy.

Pet Fact

BECOMING A VET

To become a vet, first you have to go to college and take a lot of science classes. Then you have four more years of vet school. This is when you get to work directly with animals. In your last year of vet school, you will take a special test. If you pass, you will get your license to practice veterinary medicine. Congratulations!

Snowball was Kyung's new dog. She was just a few months old.

Sam looked at the two girls and nodded. "Okay," he said. "You can keep Elliot company."

"Yay!" the girls cried.

"But first we have to ask your parents."

While Sam, Amy, and Kyung went to check with the girls' parents, Elliot sat inside the van and stared at the cloudy sky. The gray day matched his mood. All he had wanted to do this Saturday was sort through his rock collection. Instead, he was on his way to a dog shelter. Elliot would never admit it out loud, but dogs scared him a little. He sighed. It was going to be a long afternoon.

Wiggly Balls of Fur

Adopt-Your-BFF was down a steep hill, at the bottom of a valley. As soon as Sam had parked, Kyung and Amy rushed out of the van and ran inside. Elliot helped his brother. Together, they carried bags of puppy food into the small one-story building. Sam stopped at the front desk to say hi to Tina, the shelter's manager. Elliot stayed near his brother. He read a poster that hung behind the desk: *Adopt Your BFF Today!*

Kyung and Amy were already in the back area where the dogs were kept. Rows of cages were stacked on top of each other. The larger bottom cages held two big dogs. Some smaller and medium-size dogs filled the upper cages.

Kyung counted all the animals. "When I adopted Snowball, there were a lot more dogs," she said. "Now there are only seven dogs and six puppies."

Tina overheard her. "That's because we had a big adoption fair last weekend. Most of our dogs found good homes."

Amy peered into the cage with the six puppies. Three were all white, and two were tan with splotches of black.

The tiniest puppy was a pretty copper color. The puppies yipped and stepped over one another.

"They are sooo cute!" Amy cooed.

"How old are they?" Kyung asked.

"They're about ten weeks old," Sam said. He unlocked the cage.

Amy scooped up the tiny copper puppy. "This one is my favorite," she said. "I'm going to call her Penny."

Sam gently lifted a puppy with a splotch of black over its eye from the cage. "But she isn't yours," he reminded Amy. He gave Kyung the puppy to hold.

"Not yet," Amy said. "But my parents have been promising that I can get a dog someday. They just *have to* let me have her."

Elliot shook his head. He couldn't understand what the fuss was about. The puppies were cute, sure. They were wiggly balls of fur with big dark eyes. But they also demanded a lot of attention. And the one Kyung was holding had just nipped her fingers.

"Ouch!" Kyung gave the puppy back to Sam.

"Puppies this age like to bite," Sam told her. "It's natural."

"I know," Kyung said. "Snowball nipped when we first got her. But we trained her to stop."

Sam held out the black-and-tan puppy to Elliot. "Would you like to hold him?"

Elliot put up a hand. "No thanks,"

IT'S PLAYTIME!

It is important to play with your puppy for at least 20 minutes every day and give them at least 30 minutes of exercise. Playtime is a great way to bond with your puppy, and it's very fun!

he said. He didn't want a puppy gnawing on his fingers.

Sam put both puppies back in the cage with the rest of the litter. Then he opened the cage below. A big dog poked its head out and sniffed the air.

Elliot backed away.

"This is Toby," Sam said. "He's very gentle."

Toby slowly came out of the cage and thumped his bushy tail against Sam's leg.

"It's been years since Toby was a puppy," Sam said. "He was an older dog when his family left him with us."

"Why did they leave him?" Elliot asked.

"The new apartment they were moving to didn't allow pets," Sam explained.

Elliot swallowed hard. That must have been rough. He wondered if Toby missed his family.

"Toby doesn't get much attention, not the way the puppies do," Sam said. "Would you like to spend some time with him, Elliot?"

Elliot didn't answer right away. Toby was a *big* dog. He came all the way up to Sam's thigh. But Sam had said he was gentle. "Okay," he whispered.

Leaving the girls fussing over the puppies, Sam led Toby and Elliot to a quiet area in the back of the building. Toby flopped on the rug, and Elliot sat down next to him. The big dog rested his head on Elliot's knee. Elliot stroked his silky ears, and Toby let out a sigh.

A LOOK INSIDE

Most of the animals in a typical animal shelter are dogs and cats. But some shelters take in birds, rabbits, and other pets. When an animal first enters the shelter, a vet gives it a checkup. The vet will make sure the animal is healthy. If there is a problem, the vet will try to fix it.

Staff and volunteers look after the animals. They give the animals food and water and clean their cages or pens. They walk the dogs and cuddle the cats.

PICK ME!

Before you can adopt a pet, you have to fill out an application and answer questions. Then a volunteer will take you to see the animals. After you have picked out a pet, you will sign a contract. The contract says the adopter promises to take good care of the animal.

Pet Fact

"He likes it!" Elliot said, surprised.

"He sure does," Sam said.

While Elliot was petting Toby, Sam unloaded the rest of the bags of puppy food from the van. Kyung and Amy were following Tina around the shelter. She showed the girls how to scoop the right amount of puppy kibble. She even let them feed the puppies. Elliot preferred to stay with Toby. He scratched behind the dog's silky ears, and Toby wriggled and let out a big yawn. He seemed happy.

The bell on the front door tinkled, and a man walked in. He had gray hair and sad, droopy eyes. In his arms was a large cardboard box.

"Hi, Mr. Rooney," Sam said. "What's that you have?"

"Just a few things," the man said gruffly. "Some canned dog food, leashes, a few toys." He placed the box on the front desk. "They were Quincy's. I thought your place could put them to good use."

"Thanks," Tina said. "We can always use more supplies. And I'm sorry about Quincy. He was a great dog."

"Yeah, well." Mr. Rooney shrugged.

At the sound of Mr. Rooney's voice, Toby's ears perked up. The old dog lifted himself slowly off the rug. Then he ambled to Mr. Rooney's side.

"Do you want to see the new puppies?" Amy asked. "They're adorable."

"Not interested," he said quickly.

He bent down to pet Toby, then left.

Tina shook her head. "He's still upset about Quincy. He loved that dog."

"What happened?" Kyung asked.

"Mr. Rooney's dog died a few months ago," Sam said. "They did everything together."

"That's so sad," Amy said.

Tina sighed. "It is. But Quincy lived a long, happy life." She slipped on her jacket. "I have to get going," she told Sam. "Will you lock up when you leave?"

"Sure thing," Sam said. "I'm almost done with my chores. Then I have to get these kids home."

While Sam finished feeding the dogs, Elliot took the box off the counter and looked through it. There were throw toys, a tangle of leashes, and cans of dog food. At the very bottom, buried under some rawhide bones, was some kind of book. Elliot dug it out. It smelled musty, but that didn't stop him from opening it. The book was all about rocks and how to identify them. He was thumbing through the pages when Sam called to them.

"Let's get a move on, kids," he said. "It's late, and I promised Amy's and Kyung's parents I'd have them home by now."

Elliot hurried to put on his jacket. Without thinking, he slipped the book in his pocket.

Riddle Me This

On the ride home, the drizzle of rain turned into a downpour. The van's windshield wipers swished back and forth at top speed. Elliot peered out the window at the two-lane highway. He listened to Amy talk to her mother on Sam's cell phone.

"And the littlest dog was so cute," she said. "She's the one I want. Please, Mom? Pretty please?"

Elliot noticed how tightly Amy's hand gripped the phone.

"But why?" Amy cried. "You promised I could have a dog."

After some more back-and-forth, Amy said goodbye to her mother. "She said puppies are a lot of work."

"They sure are," Sam said over his shoulder.

"My mom said first I have to prove that I'm responsible enough."

Kyung patted her friend's arm. "You can help me take care of Snowball. That will show your parents that you're ready for a dog."

But Amy just shook her head and stuck out her bottom lip. "I'll never get a dog. Never." Her eyes brimmed with tears.

Elliot reached for a tissue. He twisted in his seat to hand it to Amy.

Good morning! What are the puppies doing today at the rescue center?

Arf! Arf! It's time for breakfast.

Scrub-a-dub! This puppy needs a bath.

Picture day! A photo of this sweet puppy will go on the adoption website.

Let's play! The puppies run around the fenced-in yard.

Cuddle up! These puppies found their forever family.

The hard edge of the book in his jacket poked his side. He pulled it out. Maybe there was something in the book to cheer up Amy. He flipped through the musty pages, and an old yellowed envelope fell out.

Elliot opened the envelope. Inside was a single sheet of loose-leaf paper with words hand-printed in faded purple ink. Elliot read the first two sentences: " 'Answer the riddle below. It will lead you to a great treasure.' " Underneath was a riddle.

> What do you put in a bucket to make it lighter?

"What did you say?" Kyung asked. Elliot realized he had read the riddle out loud. He repeated it. Then he showed Kyung and Amy the book and the sheet of paper.

"That's strange," Amy said, drying her eyes on her sleeve.

"What do you think the treasure is?" Kyung asked. "A precious jewel?"

"Maybe it's a chest filled with gold," Amy said.

"Or maybe it's a piece of gum," Sam said from the front seat. "It sounds like someone is pulling your leg." He stopped at a light. "Wow," he added, "this rain is really coming down."

Elliot repeated the riddle a third time. " 'What do you put in a bucket to make it lighter?' " He scratched his chin. "Any ideas?"

A VISIT TO THE VET

The vet will ask you questions about your pet's health and behavior. Is your pet eating? Is it active? Are there any problems? Next, the vet will check your pet's fur—a shiny coat means a healthy animal. Then the vet will look at your pet's eyes and ears. The eyes should be clear, and the ears, clean. A vet will also look inside your pet's mouth to make sure the teeth are in good shape. Next, the vet may listen to your pet's heart and lungs with a stethoscope. The vet will also weigh your pet and take its temperature. If it needs any shots or medicine, the vet will give them. Now the visit to the vet is over. You can take your pet home—until checkup time again next year.

"That's easy," Amy answered. "Air."

"I don't think that's it," Kyung said. "How would you put air in a bucket?"

"Besides," Elliot said, "air has weight."

"It does not," Amy said.

Elliot was about to argue when Sam pulled over and stopped the van.

"What happened?" Kyung asked.

A state trooper was walking over to them. Sam opened his window just enough to talk to the trooper without letting too much rain into the van.

"What's the problem, officer?" he asked politely. "This is some really nasty weather, isn't it?"

The trooper nodded. Rain dripped off his hat. "Yep," he said. "This storm came up all of a sudden. We weren't expecting so much rain. It caused the creek to overflow. Now the road up ahead is flooded. We just closed it. You'll have to turn around and go back the way you came."

"I'm trying to get to Greenville," Sam told him.

"Take the exit over by Pine Valley," the trooper advised. "That road is safe."

Sam thanked the officer and closed his window. Then he slowly made a U-turn and drove back in the direction they'd come.

Elliot looked out the foggy window. In front of an abandoned shed, he could see a rusty watering can. Water poured out from its spout. "A hole!" he shouted.

Amy and Kyung turned to stare at him.

"The answer to the riddle," he explained. " 'What do you put in a bucket to make it lighter?' "

"A hole!" Amy and Kyung sang out.

Elliot stared at the riddle in his hand. "But how does the answer lead to treasure?" he wondered aloud.

Dangerous Weather

After driving several miles, they were about to pass by the animal shelter. The rain was still coming down hard, and Sam was driving slowly.

"I hope the puppies are safe," Amy shouted over the sound of the rain hitting the roof and the slapping windshield wipers.

The building had been built on low ground. While the road was still safe to drive on, the water was quickly filling the valley below.

Elliot thought of Toby sleeping in the big cage below the puppies. What if the water seeped under the door and started to rise? Toby would be trapped. "We have to stop!" he cried.

His brother was already turning into the drive that led to the shelter. "The dogs are okay for now," Sam told them. "But I don't like how fast the water is rising. If the creek overruns its banks, the building will flood for sure."

"What can we do?" Kyung asked.

Sam pulled out his cell phone. "I'm calling Tina." He dialed. "Hi, Tina," he said when she answered. He explained about the rising water. "We have to get the animals out of the shelter," he told her. "It's not safe for them—or us—to stay here." He listened and nodded his head. "That's a good idea," he said. He put away his phone.

"What's a good idea?" Amy demanded.

"Tina reminded me that Frank Rooney has a cabin on high ground not far from here. It's right up the road. We can take the dogs there until the storm quiets down. Are you ready to help?"

"Yes!" all three kids shouted.

Covering their heads with their jackets, they dashed into the building and got to work. Kyung packed up the food for the dogs and puppies. Amy put the puppies into a crate, and the kids brought it to the van. Elliot helped

Sam leash the older dogs and walk them into the van. Once inside, they strapped all seven dogs into safety harnesses.

Toby was the last one in.

The rain didn't seem to bother him, but he walked slowly.

"His legs are stiff," Sam explained. "He's an old dog. When it rains like this, his joints hurt."

Elliot stroked Toby's fur and gave him a thick blanket to rest on. Then all three kids climbed into the van.

"My sneakers are soaked," Amy said.

"So are mine," Kyung said. "And my hair is wet too. I hope Mr. Rooney has a lot of towels."

"What if he isn't home?" Elliot asked.

"Don't worry," Sam said. "Tina told me he leaves a key under the mat for emergencies." He drove slowly up the steep mountain road. "And this certainly is an emergency."

FROM HERE TO THERE

It's not always easy to move an animal from one place to another. Many animals get nervous when they travel. That's why it is important to make the trip comfortable and safe for everyone.

A familiar toy helps this **KITTEN** stay calm in its carrier.

PRECIOUS CARGO

When a shelter needs to relocate a lot of animals for a better chance to find their forever homes, volunteers pitch in.

Pet Fact

This **DOG** is traveling by plane to its new home. The large, sturdy carrier helps it stay safe during the flight.

This clever **CAT** found a special way to travel. How do you think the horse feels?

HORSES ride in special trailers where they have plenty of room to move and hay to eat.

Before starting the van, Sam passed his phone to Amy. "You and Kyung need to call your parents and tell them there's been a change in plans. I don't want them to worry. Tell them that I'll drive you home after we get the dogs settled."

By the time the girls had finished speaking to their parents, the group had made the short trip up the hill to the small cabin.

Mr. Rooney was on the front porch. He had on a long raincoat, a hat, and rubber boots. He looked surprised when Sam stepped out of the van.

"What are you doing up here?" he asked.

Sam quickly filled him in on the

situation. "And so," he ended, "we hoped you would let the dogs stay in the cabin until the storm breaks."

Mr. Rooney frowned and looked at all the dogs in the back of the van. Some were barking to be let out.

"I was just going up the road," he said. "I need to check on my neighbor. Sometimes her generator goes out in storms."

"That's kind of you," Sam said.

"Well, we've been neighbors a long time," Mr. Rooney replied. "This cabin has been in my family for ages. I used to come up here when I was just a boy."

"So . . . about the dogs?" Sam asked. "They won't cause any trouble. I promise."

WALKING THE DOG

All dogs need exercise. Going on walks is a fun way to spend time with your best friend. For safety, be sure to always put a leash on your dog. And it's a good idea to bring water and a bowl with you in case your dog gets thirsty.

Pet Fact

WHAT TO WEAR?

In colder weather, dogs without thick fur might need a sweater or coat. Dogs don't need to wear anything in the summer. But you should walk your dog in the mornings or evenings when it's cooler.

Mr. Rooney stared into the back of the van. Toby's head was pressed against the back window. His tongue was out, and he was panting. "Yes, the dogs can stay. I won't be away for long."

"Thank you," Sam said.

"And I want you and the kids to stay here, too," Mr. Rooney added. "No sense in you driving in a storm like this. Here's my number if you need anything. Wait here until it passes. Then you can be on your way."

Sam nodded. "We'll do that," he said. "Sorry to cause you trouble."

"No trouble," Mr. Rooney said gruffly.

A Missing Puppy

The children helped Sam bring the dogs into the cabin. They dried off the wet animals, then themselves. Toby settled into a warm spot in front of the screened fireplace.

Sam laughed. "You stay right here, Toby, and warm your old bones." He patted the big dog's head. "Amy, you can let the puppies out of the crate. They need some exercise. I'm taking the rest of the dogs into the bedroom."

Even though the log cabin was small,

there was plenty for the puppies to do. As soon as Amy opened the crate, they dashed out. They scampered across the wood floor and began chasing each other. Amy and Kyung clapped in delight.

Elliot plopped beside Toby. The old dog kept his eyes on the frisky puppies. When one skidded into him, Toby gave the puppy a lick and nudged her away.

Kyung had a ball in her pocket. She tossed it gently, and the puppies ran after it. They chased the rolling ball all through the cabin—down the hallway, into the open kitchenette, and into the mudroom. Their excited yapping filled the cabin.

Sam came out of the bedroom. He scooped up two puppies, one in each hand. "You guys need to go back in your crate,"

he said. "You're getting too excited." He gently placed the furry balls into the crate.

"Help me get the rest of the puppies," Sam said to Kyung and Amy. Elliot stroked Toby's ears and watched Kyung and Amy chase the puppies around the room.

"Here are two more," Kyung said.

"And I have another," Amy said. She scrunched her nose. "But shouldn't there be one more? Where's Penny, the tiny copper puppy?"

Sam counted the puppies in the crate. Five. One puppy was missing. "She must be hiding," he said. "All hands on deck. You, too, Elliot. We have to find her."

Sam and the kids searched the cabin. No puppy.

"Where can she be?" Amy wailed.

Kyung bit her lip. She looked like she wanted to say something.

Sam looked puzzled. "Amy," he said, "at the shelter, you put the puppies in the crate. Are you sure you got all of them?"

TALK THIS WAY

NEIGH!
"Here I am!
Pay attention
to me!"

Animals can't speak, of course. But that doesn't mean they don't communicate. Your pet may be telling you something important. You just have to know how to listen.

**SQUEAK!
SQUEAK!**
"Feed me!"

Your cat purrs when it is relaxed and happy. Squeaks mean your guinea pig wants food, and chirps and whistles mean it's happy to see you. A dog may bark as a warning. It will also bark to let you know it needs something—a walk or a favorite toy. Or maybe it's time for dinner.

HISS!
"Go away!"

"I think so," Amy said. "But we were in a hurry. There was so much going on. I can't remember if I counted them."

"I don't think you did," Kyung whispered.

Amy looked stricken. "What if the puppy is still at the shelter?"

Another Riddle

Sam hurried over to the coatrack. He put on one of Mr. Rooney's spare rain jackets. "It wasn't your fault," he told Amy. "We were all in a hurry. I should have checked the crate too." He zipped up his jacket. "I'll drive back to the shelter and see if the puppy is there."

Amy gasped. "What do you mean *if*?" she asked. "The puppy has to be at the shelter. Where else could she be?"

"I don't remember seeing her in the

cage," Kyung said. "Do you?"

Amy shook her head, and her lower lip trembled. "I don't remember!"

"Don't worry," Sam said, patting her on the shoulder. "We'll find her. The shelter is just down the road. I won't be long."

"Can't we go with you?" Amy begged. "We can help you find her."

"No," said Sam. "Mr. Rooney will be back soon. But until he's here, I need you to stay and look after the dogs. The telephone is over there." He pointed to an old-fashioned phone on the desk in the hallway. "Call me if there's a problem. You know my number, Elliot."

After Sam left, the three kids stared at each other. They were all thinking the same thing: where was the missing puppy—and was she okay?

Outside, the wind howled. A flash of lightning lit up the gloom. It was followed quickly by a loud crack.

The three kids jumped.

"It was probably just a falling tree branch," Elliot said bravely. He hoped he sounded calmer than he felt. His heart was racing. Kyung and Amy were clinging to each other.

"Let's search one more time," Elliot suggested. He figured that being busy would keep their minds off the storm. "Remember how the puppies were running around? Maybe the puppy got stuck somewhere."

"Good idea," said Kyung. "Let's look for her together, Amy."

But Amy shook her head. "It's my fault," she said in a low voice. "My mom is right. I'm not responsible enough to have a dog."

Kyung hugged her friend. "That's not what she said. She said you have to *show* her you're responsible. So start looking."

Amy nodded, and the three kids examined every inch of the cabin. They looked behind the refrigerator and stove. They crawled under tables and opened cupboards. But they didn't find the puppy.

Elliot sank on the rug next to Toby. The big dog licked his hand. "I guess she's not here," Elliot said at last.

Kyung nodded.

• WEATHER OR NOT? •

With their extra-sharp senses, some animals may be able to anticipate weather changes before we do. A dog can hear rumblings of thunder long before the sound reaches our ears, and it may bark or hide. How do other animals behave when bad weather is coming?

SHEEP run when frightened. But they often huddle together during bad weather.

BIRDS sense air pressure changes that signal a storm is on the way, and they fly low to avoid strong winds.

FROGS croak more loudly and longer when bad weather is coming to attract potential mates.

COWS lie down to stay warm. This often happens when the temperature drops before a rainstorm.

"Then why hasn't Sam called to say he's found her?" Amy's dark eyes were wide with worry.

Elliot wished he could get everyone's mind off the puppy. Then he remembered the paper with the riddle. He pulled it from his jeans pocket and unfolded it. "I still don't get how the riddle leads to treasure," he said.

Kyung looked around the cabin. "The book was in the box of supplies Mr. Rooney brought to the shelter, right?"

Elliot nodded.

"Then maybe the treasure is somewhere in the cabin. Didn't he say the cabin has been in his family for years and years?"

Amy stood up. "The answer to the riddle was a hole in a bucket." She walked over to a framed print hanging on the wall. It showed a girl with a bucket milking a cow. Amy peered at the picture. "There's a tiny hole in the bucket," she said excitedly. "It looks like it was made with a pin."

Kyung and Elliot got up to look.

Amy took the print off the wall and turned it over. A piece of notebook paper was folded and taped to the other side.

"What are you waiting for?" Kyung cried. "Open it and see what it says."

Bad News

Amy carefully removed the yellowed strip of tape. Then she unfolded the paper. "This note is written in purple ink, too," she said.

"Read it!" Elliot said.

" 'Good for you,' " Amy read. " 'You found the answer to the riddle. Now here is another one.' "

> What has eighty-eight keys but can't open any doors?

Elliot shook his head. "It beats me.

What good are keys if you can't open a door?"

"Keys aren't just for opening doors," Amy reminded him. "There are keys that open safes or diaries."

"Good thinking," Elliot said.

Kyung giggled.

"What's so funny?" Amy asked her friend.

"I can't believe you don't know the answer," Kyung said.

"You do?" Elliot said.

"Of course," Kyung said.

"Well, are you going to tell us what it is?" Amy tapped her foot impatiently.

"It's a piano!" Kyung sang out proudly. "I should know. I take lessons on one every week."

STORM PREP

Big storms can seem scary for people and pets. The best way to get through them is to stay calm and be prepared. Here are some tips to keep you and your family safe the next time a storm hits.

- If your pet is afraid of storms, talk to your vet about ways to help it cope.

- During a storm, stay indoors and away from windows.

- Listen for weather alerts and updates on your radio or TV.

- Have batteries and flashlights on hand in case the power goes out.

- Keep a first aid kit in the house and car. Some items to include are bandages, scissors, medicine, hand sanitizer, safety pins, and a blanket.

- Keep a packed overnight bag handy in case you need to leave quickly. Think about what you'll need, such as pajamas, a book, and clothes. And don't forget a bag for pets that includes food and water, bowls, and a leash or travel crate.

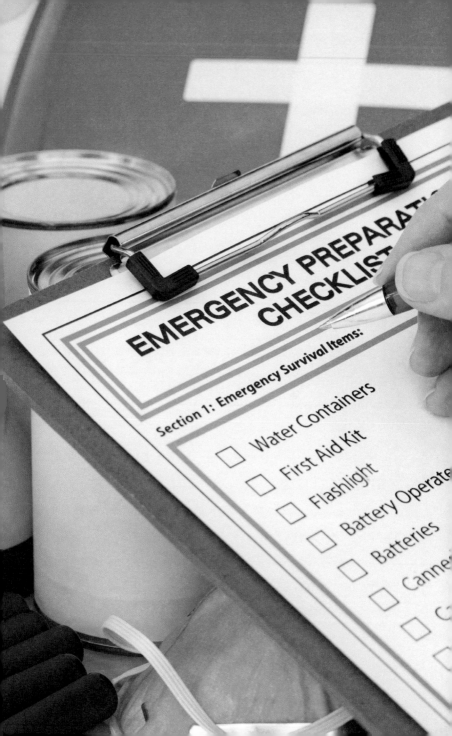

EMERGENCY PREPARATION CHECKLIST

Section 1: Emergency Survival Items:

- ☐ Water Containers
- ☐ First Aid Kit
- ☐ Flashlight
- ☐ Battery Operate
- ☐ Batteries
- ☐ Canne
- ☐ C

Elliot groaned. It seemed so obvious now.

But Amy wasn't satisfied. "What kind of clue is that?" she demanded. "Look around. Do you see a piano?"

It was true. A piano couldn't fit in the small cabin.

Just then the telephone rang. Elliot stepped over to the desk and picked up the receiver. "Hello?" He listened for a long time.

"Okay," he said at last. "Don't worry about us. We're okay." He hung up the phone.

"That was Sam," he told the girls. "The puppy wasn't at the shelter."

Amy shook her head. "That can't be," she said. "Where else could she be?

• WHERE CAN IT BE? •

Everybody loses things. Maybe you lost your glasses or your favorite pen. Or maybe you can't find the homework that's due on Monday. The first thing to do is to stay calm. Take a deep breath and clear your mind.

STEP 1

Try to remember when you last had the object.

STEP 2

Retrace your steps.

STEP 3

If you still can't find what you're looking for, ask other people. Maybe they know where it is.

STEP 4

Still no luck? Then take a break. Sometimes when you stop looking for a lost object, that's when you find it.

She's not here. We looked and looked."

Another bolt of lightning filled the room. It was followed by thunder.

"What if she's outside in the storm?" Amy cried.

Kyung put her arms around her friend. "When will Sam be back?" she asked.

"That's the other problem," Elliot said. "His van stalled in all this rain. He's trying to fix it, but he said it might be awhile."

Kyung gulped. "I'm getting scared," she confessed. "I just want to go home."

"But what about Penny?" Amy said. "We have to find her."

"Sam called Mr. Rooney and told him about the missing puppy and the van. Mr. Rooney is on his way. He should be here in about ten minutes," Elliot said. "Maybe he'll have some ideas."

CRASH!

Outside, a tree branch fell.

Amy clutched Kyung's arm. "I hope he gets here soon," she said.

Elliot didn't answer. He was staring at something on the desk. Next to the phone was a gold music box in the shape of a piano. He picked it up and showed it to the girls. "Here's the piano."

The Final Riddle

Elliot turned the music box upside down. But there wasn't a piece of paper taped to the bottom.

"Open the lid," Kyung said.

Elliot did. "I don't see anything," he said. He showed them the smooth red velvet under the lid.

"I don't care about this silly game!" Amy cried. "I just want to find Penny." She went and gazed into the crate.

The five puppies were sleeping in a pile. Amy looked at them and sighed.

Kyung took the music box from Elliot. "I have one of these," she said. She gently lifted the velvet compartment. Underneath, next to the mechanism that played the musical notes, was a small folded piece of paper. Carefully, Kyung took it out and handed it to Elliot.

Taking a deep breath, Elliot read the riddle.

> This is the last riddle. If you succeed, you will find the treasure. What has hands but cannot clap?

Amy looked up from the puppies. "Read that again," she demanded.

WRITE A RIDDLE

A riddle is a puzzling question that needs to be solved. Would you like to make your own riddle? Here's how:

First, decide what the answer to your riddle will be. It can be an animal or an object or a place—anything.

Then make a list of words that describe your answer.

Write a sentence for each word.

Now give your riddle to a friend. Can your friend solve the riddle?

For example, if you picked a squirrel as your answer, your riddle might look like this:

It's an animal.
It has a bushy tail.
It likes to eat acorns.
It lives in the forest.
What is it?

Elliot repeated, " 'What has hands but cannot clap?' "

"I know," Amy said. Her eyes lit up. "It's a clock, right? It has to be a clock."

"Yes!" Kyung said. "That makes sense."

"So where's a clock?" Elliot asked.

The three kids looked around the cabin. A wall clock hung in the kitchenette. But when they took it down, nothing was taped to it.

"Maybe it's *inside* the clock," Amy said.

Elliot shook his head. "I don't want to break Mr. Rooney's clock."

"I think I remember seeing another clock," Kyung said. "It was when we were looking for the puppy." She walked over to the mudroom at the back of the cabin.

Amy and Elliot followed her.

A tall grandfather clock stood against one wall. The base of the clock had a small door. Kyung crouched and opened it.

Elliot and Amy held their breath.

Kyung shook her head. "It's empty," she reported. "Maybe someone already found the treasure a long time ago."

Elliot nodded. He felt disappointed. They had solved all the riddles but hadn't found the treasure. He walked over to the back window and looked out onto the garden. "The storm finally stopped," he said. "It's just drizzling now."

"Yay!" Kyung shouted.

Amy held up her hand. "Be quiet!" she ordered. "I heard something."

The three kids listened. Faint but steady yapping came from the clock.

"That's strange," Kyung said. "A clock that barks?"

"That's not the clock!" Amy cried. "That's the puppy!" She dropped to her knees and stuck her head in the open compartment. "Penny, where are you?"

A louder yap answered her.

"Maybe she's *behind* the clock," Elliot said. "Help me move it."

Carefully, the three children inched the giant clock farther away from the wall. No puppy.

"But I can hear her!" Amy wailed.

Elliot shook his head. "The yapping isn't coming from the clock," he said. "Listen."

OH NO!

Puppies are curious and like to explore. This is especially true when they find themselves in new places. They may jump up on furniture and counters, chew your favorite shoes, steal food, and bite and tug on things and people. They need plenty of exercise and training to outgrow these puppy behaviors. And just like young children, they need to be watched so they don't get into trouble.

Puppies and kids love to be messy together!

The children stood still, not talking.

Yap! Yap! Yap!

"It's coming from inside the wall!" Kyung shouted.

Elliot examined the paneled wall around the clock carefully. Every few feet he knocked on the wood.

"What are you doing?" Amy asked.

"Shh," Elliot said. "I need to find where the wall isn't solid." A few feet from the clock, he knocked again. Instead of a dull thud, the sound was hollow.

"This is it!" he cried. He pointed to a narrow door that came up to his waist. The door blended in so well with the wood that it was almost impossible to see.

"It's a trapdoor," he explained. "I bet it goes to the attic. We have one at our house."

"But how did Penny get in there?" Amy asked.

Elliot shrugged. "She must have managed to open the door with her paw."

"I see scratches in the wood," Kyung said. She pointed to faint marks at the bottom of the door.

Elliot nodded. "And it's pretty drafty in here. The wind might have slammed the door shut and trapped her inside."

"Just get her out!" Amy wailed.

There wasn't a doorknob. So Elliot felt around the wood panels until he found an opening. He wedged his fingers

inside and pulled. The door popped open.
Out sprang a yapping furry ball.

Amy scooped the tiny, trembling
puppy into her arms. "Penny!" she cried.

CHAPTER 9

Treasure at Last

Penny was licking Amy's face when the back door opened.

Mr. Rooney stepped into the mudroom. He looked at the grandfather clock and the opened trapdoor and frowned. But he didn't say a word.

Elliot scrambled to his feet. "We can explain, Mr. Rooney," he said.

"I'm sure you can," Mr. Rooney said. He took off his raincoat and hat and placed them on hooks. "But first I need a hot cup of cocoa. What about you?"

Ten minutes later, the children were sipping hot cocoa. They told Mr. Rooney about their adventures.

Mr. Rooney chuckled. "You found the envelope in my old book?"

Elliot showed him the first riddle.

"I can remember writing this," Mr. Rooney told them.

Amy looked up from petting Penny. "*You* wrote the riddles?"

"Yes," Mr. Rooney said. "When I was not much older than you. My cousin Tim was visiting, and I thought it would amuse him."

"So Tim never found the treasure?" Kyung asked.

Mr. Rooney shook his head. "All Tim

wanted to do was fish and play cards." He shrugged. "So I tucked away the envelope in the book I was reading and forgot all about it."

"So where is the treasure?" Kyung asked. "We didn't find any."

"Yes, we did," Amy said sharply. She picked up Penny and gave her a kiss. "We found the most important treasure of all."

"That, you did," Mr. Rooney said with a smile. "But there *is* another treasure."

Elliot jumped to his feet and ran to the mudroom. The girls followed.

Elliot poked his head inside the trapdoor. "I don't see anything," he said.

"That's because you're not looking in

the right place," Mr. Rooney told him. "Remember the last riddle."

"But the treasure wasn't in the grandfather clock," Kyung said.

Elliot stared at the tall clock. Then he dragged a chair over to it. He climbed up and stood on tiptoes. He reached up and felt around the top of the clock.

"I got it!" he cried.

Mr. Rooney helped him bring down a battered cardboard box. "Open it," Mr. Rooney said.

Elliot lifted the lid. Inside, it was packed with objects from nature: rocks with glittery specks in them, dried leaves, pine cones, and many other wonders.

TREASURE HUNTING

It can be lots of fun to go treasure hunting in your backyard or neighborhood. Make sure to bring a camera with you to take pictures of anything that catches your eye. You can also bring a notebook to make notes about where you found the treasures, but make sure you leave everything where you found it!

"Everything I collected came from the woods around the cabin," Mr. Rooney said proudly.

Elliott picked up a shiny rock and examined it closely. "I collect rocks, too," he said.

Mr. Rooney picked up the box and handed it to Elliot. "Then you should have this," he said.

"I can't take it!" Elliot said. "It's yours."

"But you played my game and won."

"We all did," Elliot said. "Kyung and Amy solved the riddles too." He turned to the two girls. "We could share it," he said shyly.

"No, thank you," Amy said. "I already have my treasure." She snuggled Penny.

Kyung kneeled beside Elliott.
"I'd like to share," she said. "I collect leaves."

"Great!" Elliot smiled at her.

•ADOPTION OPTIONS•

When you go to an animal shelter to adopt a pet, it's easy to fall in love with all the animals. It can be hard to make a decision. So before you go, discuss with your family what you're looking for in an animal companion. Then shelter workers can help match you up with the perfect pet for you.

PUPPY

Puppies are high energy! They tend to cause or get into trouble. And they need to be house-trained. Does your family have the time and patience for a puppy?

TEENAGER

Dogs become "teenagers" at around six months. This may last for a few months or a year. These youngsters like to explore the world. They can sometimes be unpredictable and may still need some training.

ADULT

Dogs are considered grown-ups at one or two years old. They retain their curiosity and energy, but are more calm. Most can fit into family life easily.

SENIOR

Older dogs make wonderful companions. They may develop medical issues that need attention, but mostly they want to love and be loved.

Pet Fact

DECEMBER

2

National Mutt Day!

WHAT'S A MUTT?

Mutts are unique mixes of multiple breeds. Many people think mutts are likely to be healthier in the long run. Purebred dogs have traits that are specific to a particular breed.

More Surprises

The rest of the afternoon passed quickly. Sam returned. He had fixed the van, but many roads were still flooded. Mr. Rooney invited them to stay until it was safe to drive.

Sam was surprised and happy to see Penny curled up in Amy's lap. The children told him how they had rescued the puppy from her hiding place.

"You were all very responsible," Sam said. "I'm proud of you."

SUPERSIZE!
No matter how big your puppy gets, it may still try to fit on your lap.

After they fed and walked all the dogs, Mr. Rooney popped some popcorn. Then he sat in his easy chair and told them stories about when he was a boy. Many of his stories were about the fun he'd had exploring the woods and the treasures he had found there.

He told the children about all the animals he had spotted, including a friendly chipmunk that lived in the woodpile. As he talked, Toby came over and rested his snout on his knee. Mr. Rooney petted the old dog. Every now and then, he sneaked him a piece of popcorn.

Sam stepped outside to call Kyung's and Amy's parents. When he came back into the cabin, he told the children it was time to go. The roads they would travel on were safe to drive.

"But we're having so much fun!" Amy said.

Mr. Rooney smiled. "You can come back and visit anytime."

The children cheered.

Everyone worked together to get the dogs settled in the back of the van. Toby was the last to leave.

Elliot clipped on the dog's leash and started for the door. Mr. Rooney took the leash from him. "That's okay, Elliot," Mr. Rooney said. "I already spoke to Sam and Tina. Toby will be staying with me from now on."

"Really?"

Mr. Rooney nodded. "I forgot how much I missed having a dog. After Quincy died, I thought I'd never have a place in my heart for another animal." He stroked Toby's head. "But Toby and I seem to get along."

Elliot smiled. He knew that Toby would have a good home with Mr.

Rooney. He crouched and looked into the dog's dark-brown eyes. "Goodbye, Toby," he said. "Next time I come, I'll bring you a special treat."

When the van pulled up to the shelter, there was a car already in the parking lot. It had a Maine license plate. A tall man and two children, a girl and a boy, got out. The man shook Sam's hand. "My name is Thomas Cardozo," he said. "And this is Maddie and Atticus."

"Yes," Sam said. "You called earlier to say you were dropping by."

"That's right," said Mr. Cardozo. "We're on our way home from a family vacation. When we stopped in a restaurant in town to wait out the storm, the waitress told us about your shelter. We looked up your website and—"

"We saw a photo of the new puppies!" Maddie exclaimed. "We *really* want to adopt one."

"Have you had any experience with taking care of puppies?" Sam asked.

"Oh yes," said Atticus. "We helped take care of a dog last summer."

"He was always getting into trouble," Maddie said. "But we miss him."

"I told the kids we could adopt a puppy when we got home," their father said. "But when we saw the puppies on the website, we thought we'd stop in."

"First things first," Sam said. "We have to get the dogs settled. Then you can pick a puppy, and we'll do the paperwork."

Everybody pitched in, and soon the dogs were back inside the shelter.

Maddie peered into the cage holding the litter of puppies. "That's a cute one,"

she said. She pointed straight to Penny.

"What do you think, Atticus?"

Atticus nodded. "I like her."

·YOUR NEW PUPPY·

It's an exciting day when you bring a puppy into your home. But wait! Are you prepared?

🐾 A cozy bed inside a crate provides a safe place for the puppy to sleep when you're not around.

- Your puppy will also need a collar, a leash, and an ID tag that has your address and telephone number on it.

- Puppies need special food so they grow strong.

- Puppies love to play, so you'll need lots of toys.

- Find a vet and schedule a visit right away. A healthy puppy is a happy puppy.

- Set up a schedule. Who will feed the puppy? When will she eat? Who will house train her? When will she go outside? You will need to discuss these questions with your family. It's a good idea to make a chart that lists who is responsible for what.

And most of all, a puppy needs . . . YOU!

Amy's bottom lip began to quiver. She blinked back tears.

Sam took Penny from the cage.

Amy's tears spilled over.

Maddie reached for the puppy.

"I'm sorry," Sam said. "This one is already taken."

"It is?" Maddie said.

"It is?" Amy said.

Sam nodded. "But you can choose any of the others."

Maddie and Atticus picked the puppy with the splotch over its eye. They went to wait in the back office for Sam.

"So who is adopting Penny?" Amy asked. Her voice wobbled.

Sam placed the puppy in her arms. "You are," he said. "I spoke to your parents earlier. I told them how responsible you were with the dogs. They agreed to let you have Penny. Unless you'd like a different one?"

"No!" Amy cried. "Penny is the only dog for me." She hugged her new pet, and the puppy nibbled her finger.

"Yay!" Kyung said. "Now we both have dogs."

Amy turned to Elliot. "Why don't you adopt a puppy?" she asked. "Then our puppies could play together when we hang out."

"We're going to hang out?" he said.

"Of course," Amy said. "We're friends now. Didn't you know?"

Elliot hadn't known. But he was glad to have Amy and Kyung as friends.

Bye!

BE A VOLUNTEER!

There are many ways you can help animals. Here are just a few ideas to get you started.

Raise money for organizations that aid animals, such as rescue centers and pet shelters. Organize a bake sale or a yard sale and donate the money to your favorite animal charity.

Animal hospitals, vets, and pet shelters often need help caring for animals. You and a parent or guardian can volunteer to clean out dirty cages, feed the animals, or take dogs for walks.

Organize a pet-food drive. Shelters and rescue centers need food to feed all the animals they care for.

"So what about getting a dog?"
Kyung said.

Elliot shook his head. "I don't think
so." He looked around at the animals
in their cages and thought of Toby. "So
many of the dogs here don't have homes
yet. I'm going to come to the shelter and
spend time with them." He opened his
arms wide. "That way they'll *all* be my
dogs!"

"Yay!" cried Kyung. "I'll come too."

"Count me in," Amy said.

Sam grinned. "It looks like
Adopt-Your-BFF just got three new
volunteers."

ADOPT
ME